For the extremely fantastic
Emily Ford, with thanks
—E. W.

For Eleanor
—B. D.

Henry Holt and Company, *Publishers since 1866* • Henry Holt® is a registered
trademark of Macmillan Publishing Group, LLC • 175 Fifth Avenue, New York, NY 10010 •
mackids.com • Text copyright © 2016 by Elli Woollard • Illustrations copyright © 2016 by
Benji Davies • All rights reserved. • Library of Congress Cataloging-in-Publication Data
is available. • ISBN 978-1-250-15020-2 • Our books may be purchased in bulk for promotional,
educational, or business use. Please contact your local bookseller or the Macmillan Corporate and Premium
Sales Department at (800) 221-7945 ext. 5442 or by e-mail at MacmillanSpecialMarkets@macmillan.com. •
First published in the United Kingdom by Macmillan UK, 2016 • First American edition, 2018 • Printed in China by
Shenzhen Wing King Tong Paper Products Co Ltd, Guangdong Province • 10 9 8 7 6 5 4 3 2 1

ELLI
WOOLLARD

BENJI
DAVIES

The DRAGON and the NIBBLESOME KNIGHT

GODWINBOOKS

Henry Holt and Company · New York

The Dragons of Dread were a terrible bunch!
They ate boys for their breakfast and girls for their lunch.
But their best things of all, their favorite delights,
were dribblesome, nibblesome, knobble-kneed knights.

When the smallest of all the dragons turned four,
his parents said, "Dram, you're a baby no more!
This nest's getting cramped and you've never once flown.
Now go bite a nibblesome knight of your own!"

So Dram stretched his wings and he started to flap.
But the lightning went FLASH!
and the thunder went CLAP!

It hailed and it galed and the winds looped and curled.
And they whisked Dram away to the end of the world,

where he thumped and he bumped
and went bounce, clatter, CRASH!

And he fell in a lake
with a fountainous . . .

SPLASH!

Now, watching the skies by the edge of the shore
was young James, who had not seen a dragon before.
And he cried, "What was that? It's some rare kind of duck!
It seems to be hurt. What to do? What bad luck!"

So he took off his armor and said with a grin,

"I'm coming to help you!" and waded right in.

"A lad?" muttered Dram. "Well, he might taste all right.
Though my mom said I must nab a nibblesome knight."
And he stretched out a claw, then suddenly stopped.
His leg was all bent and his paw simply flopped.

"Oh duckie!" cried James. "Why, you poor injured thing!
Sit yourself down and I'll make you a sling."

That's better! thought Dram. *Now I must find a bite
of a dribblesome, nibblesome, knobble-kneed knight.
So he waved a goodbye, and he tried to breathe smoke,
but all that came out was a hoarse kind of croak.*

"Oh duckie!" cried James as Dram struggled to roar.
"What a strange sort of quack. Why, your throat must be sore!
Come to the woods and I'll fetch you some honey.
It's good medicine, all soothing and runny."

That's better! thought Dram. *Now I must find a bite
of a dribblesome, nibblesome, knobble-kneed knight.*
So he waved goodbye and started to fly,
but his wings were too weak to take off in the sky.

"Oh duckie!" cried James. "I'm so dreadfully rude!
You must feel quite faint—let me get you some food.
Come to the orchard. We'll soon fill our tums
full of pears and pink peaches and big purple plums."

"That's better," yawned Dram.
"Now I must find a bite . . ."
But he fell fast asleep
in the moon-marbled night.

In the morning Dram woke and said, "Hey, I feel fine!
Soon a bite of a nibblesome knight will be mine!"
And he bellowed out billions of billowing flames,
then he thought, *I'll say 'bye to that little lad James.*

TODAY:
SCHOOL
SPORTS
DAY!
WITH
SPECIAL GUESTS
THE DRAGONS OF DREAD

So he strode down the road
and he stomped through the field . . .

. . . and there was young James
with a sword and a shield!

"You're a knight?" shouted Dram.
"You're not simply a lad?"

"You're a dragon?" yelled James.
"You're all beastly and bad?"

"Yes," muttered Dram.
"I suppose I should bite."

"Oh!" mumbled James.

"Then I guess I should fight. . . .

It must be all over. The finish.

The end!"

Then they both said at once, "But I can't—
YOU'RE MY FRIEND!"

"My friend!" chortled James
as he put down his sword.

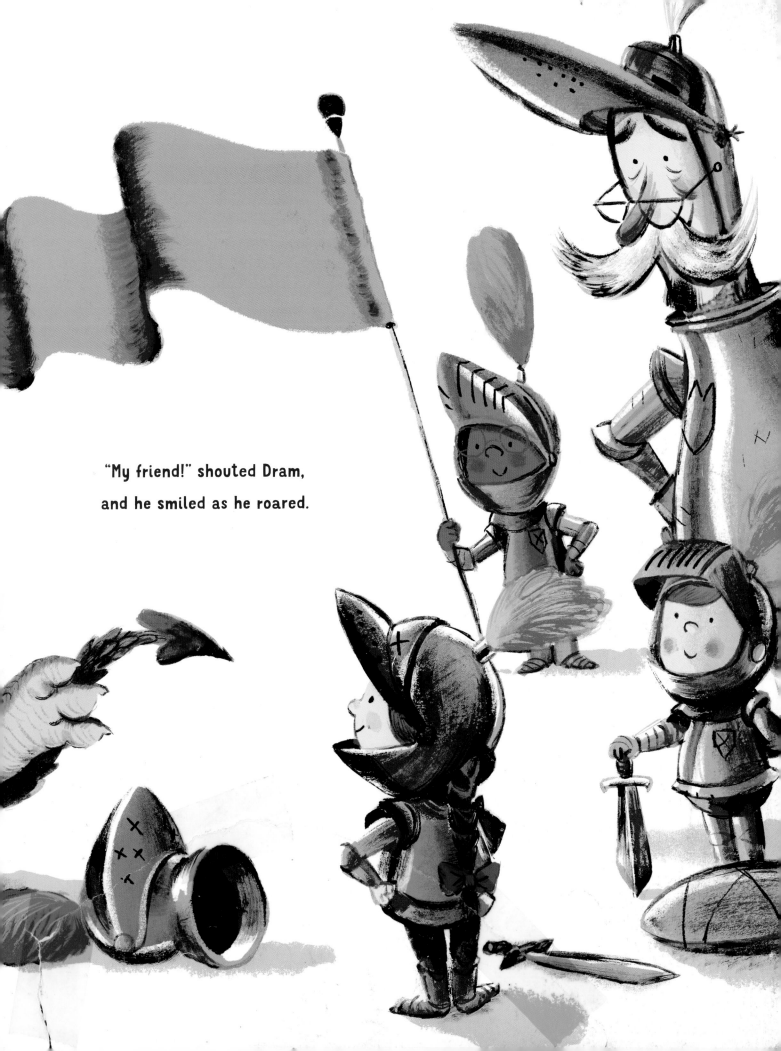

"My friend!" shouted Dram,
and he smiled as he roared.

The knights all said, "Dragons, they're not simply beasts."
The dragons said, "Knights aren't so nice for our feasts.

Nibble at knights? Why, of course we do not!"

Though every so often, they sort of . . .

...forgot.